Robbers in the House

*In the heart of old Dublin, six children discover
a thrilling new place to play, the old Fruit and
Vegetable Markets, now being demolished.*

*But what are two suspicious-looking men
doing there?*

*Why are they combing the place with
something that looks like a vacuum cleaner?*

*Is there treasure there – and can the children
find it first?*

*Their search leads them into danger,
imprisonment in an old disused mill and escape,
and there is an exciting chase through the city
streets by night, before, with the help of Patchie
their dog, all is resolved happily – and
profitably.*

Carolyn Swift

Robbers in the House

Illustrated by Terry Myler

ACORN BOOKS
The Children's Press

To Grainne
who used to skip to Jelly on the Plate
— and to all those who still do,
this book is dedicated

First published in 1981 by
The Children's Press Limited,
45 Palmerston Road, Dublin 6.
Reprinted 1989

© Text Carolyn Swift
© Illustrations The Children's Press

Published with the assistance
of the Arts Council.

ISBN 0 900068 59 0

Typesetting by Computertype.
Printed in Ireland by Mount Salus Press.

Contents

1 *Jelly on the Plate*

The Square was the best place in Dublin to play
and the families living there knew it. The grass in
the middle made a fine football pitch and the end
wall of the houses on the south side was just right
for playing ball games like Plainy-Clappy. A row of
little posts stopped cars from driving through, so it
was safe to play on the roads. Anyone could tell that
at a glance, because the roads were always covered
in little chalked 'beds', and the Square echoed to
the sound of hopping feet and the scraping of shoe-
polish tins filled with clay being kicked from one
'bed' to another.

Over the tops of the little yellow brick houses
towered the great dome of the Four Courts, where
judges sat and listened to the barristers defending
their clients and arguing over points of law.

The River Liffey flowed past the front of the Four
Courts. No ships sailed up as far as there now.
Instead there was the endless flow of trucks and lor-
ries driving along the quays, up one side and down
the other. The Square was like a quiet island in the
middle of the great sea of the city.

At least, that was how it seemed to May Byrne
one evening as she left the noisy bustle of the city
behind her and turned in to the north side of the

Square where she lived with her parents and three brothers.

As she reached the corner of the Square, she overtook old Danny Noonan. It was not hard to overtake him because of his arthritis. It made his joints stiff so that he moved slowly and awkwardly along, clutching the books he had got out of the Public Library.

Danny had been a sailor since he was fourteen but, now that he was old and crippled, he had come back to live in the Square where he had been born and reared. He could no longer bend and stretch, so the women in the Square would take turns helping him with the housework. This gave Danny lots of time for reading.

When the weather was warm enough he would bring out a chair from the front parlour and sit in the sun with his book. May and her elder brother Richie and their friends would ask him to tell them stories, because Danny knew more stories than anyone else.

Some of his stories were about the ships he had sailed on and the places he had been in his voyages. Others were stories he had read in books or had heard himself when he had been a boy. His favourite stories were about Dublin and, in particular, the Square and the streets around it.

'This is the real ould Dublin,' he would say. 'The first bridge across the Liffey was just the other side of the Four Courts. Long before O'Connell Street and the city centre were built, there were people living and working here. Baile Atha Cliath, the town of the ford of the hurdles, they called it.'

He would shake his head sadly.

'You'd want to look well at it now, before they have it all pulled down. Next thing you know, they'll have the Square down about our ears.'

'They wouldn't, would they, Danny?' said May shocked. 'They wouldn't ever pull down the Square.'

'Didn't they knock Fishamble Street on the other side of the river, and Benny's little cobbler's shop that had been his father's and his father's before him?'

'You mean, where they're buildin' the offices for the Corpo?' asked Richie. 'On Wood Quay?'

Danny nodded. 'The very place. Where they dug up all them Viking bones and bits of shoes and knives and combs. And now they're knocking down the old Fruit and Vegetable Market right beside us.'

'They had to move the Market outa the city,' said Whacker. 'The streets in Mary's Abbey was too narrow for the big container trucks of bananas and oranges.'

Whacker was Richie's friend from across the Square and he knew everything. If he had not heard his father say it, he had heard it on the radio or seen it on television.

Danny nodded again. 'And I suppose now they'll be throwing up more office blocks where once the ould Abbey stood.'

'There really was an Abbey then?' May had always wondered why a street should be called Mary's Abbey. 'Do you remember when it was there, Danny?'

Danny raised an eyebrow. 'I may be old, but I'm not that old. It was King Henry the Eighth – the one that had all the wives – broke that up. All that's left of it now is one room they found down under a warehouse, about ten or fifteen years ago.'

'How could it be under it?' asked Richie. 'D'you mean, under the ground?'

'You have it now,' said Danny, 'six feet under. It was on account of the litter.' Seeing their blank faces, he went on, 'There was that much rubbish thrown around that the ground riz higher and higher.'

'Were you ever in the bit of the Abbey that's left?'

Danny shook his head.

'I'd never get my old bones down all them steps. There's many a time I wished I could, on account of all the history that went on there. It was in that very room, the Chapter House they call it, that Silken Thomas threw down the great Sword of State because they told him his father had been done to death in the Tower of London and, d'you know what … ?'

There was a dramatic pause before he went on.

'It was all lies they told him. His father hadn't been done to death at all. But they wanted to make

him angry, the way he'd turn agin the government.
So he started the rebellion, right then and there in
that very room ... and you know how that ended.'

They nodded. They had learned, in history class,
of the tragic end of Silken Thomas, but knowing
that it had all happened only a few yards from the
Square made it seem so much more interesting. It
was like that with all Danny's stories.

After tea May ran out to join her friend Maura
Riley and Whacker's sister, Imelda, who were skipping in the corner of the square. Maura and Imelda
turned the rope while May skipped, singing one of
the rhymes her mother had sung when she was a
girl, and that her mother's mother had sung before
her and her mother before that.

> *Jelly on the plate,*
> *Jelly on the plate,*
> *Wibbly wobbly, wibbly wobbly,*
> *Jelly on the plate.*

As May chanted, she wriggled her body on the
'wibbly wobblies'. Then she went on to the next bit.

> *Money on the floor,*
> *Money on the floor,*
> *Pick it up, pick it up,*
> *Money on the floor.*

As she sang she tipped the ground, without

catching her foot in the rope, to pick up the imaginary money. Then she went on to the next bit.

> *Robbers in the house,*
> *Robbers in the house,*
> *Kick them out! Kick them out!*
> *Robbers in the house.*

This time she skipped on one foot only, kicking out the other in front of her as if to speed the robbers with a good boot on their behinds. She had reached the last verse without mishap

> *Three chips in the pan,*
> *Three chips in the pan,*
> *Turn them over, turn them ...*

But as she began to turn, a football came sailing across the Square, knocking the rope sideways so that she caught her foot in it. Richie, Whacker and Richie's other friend, Mickser Dolan, had been kicking it around on the grass. May angrily rounded on Mickser, who ran after the ball.

'Hey you, Specky Four Eyes! Mind where you're kickin' that ball! ' she shouted, snatching up the ball before Mickser could reach it.

'You broke up our game, see how you like having your own broke up!' Then she raced away from him, with Imelda and Maura following. As they reached the corner of the Square, she glanced back over her shoulder. As she expected, the three boys were chasing after them.

The rush-hour traffic was long over. There was only a lone cyclist on the road as they dashed across Mary's Abbey and on along St. Michan's Street, which divided the two sections of what had once been the Markets.

'They're catchin' up on us,' gasped Maura, as they turned into Mary's Lane. There in front of them was the huge pillared gateway to the Markets, with the coat-of-arms of Dublin city on the top.

'Quick!' panted May, 'In there!'

The gate was barred now by a tall wooden hoarding, but there was a gap in it big enough for a small person to squeeze through.

'You know we're not allowed!' cried Maura, her eyes wide. 'It's dangerous! Mammy says we'll fall down a hole and come out in Australia!'

'Then stay and be caught,' snapped Imelda. Sometimes she secretly thought Maura was a drag on the great adventures she and May would have had by themselves, but May was always loyal to Maura.

Imelda squeezed in after May. Maura hesitated; then she plunged in too and stood beside them, her heart thudding as they listened to the boys racing past.

'They've stopped by the gate!' reported May, peeping out. 'They know well we couldn't be gone far. Now they're lookin' up the lane.'

'They won't be long findin' us,' said Imelda, 'We'd better hide.'

But where? The wooden partitions and timber offices had all been torn down, leaving nothing but a big empty space the length of the block. It was like the big, dark, empty hangar Maura had looked into the time they had been taken to Dublin Airport as a holiday outing.

The overhead lights that used to hang from metal struts had all been taken down. The glass roof had been ripped out. The hoardings across the four great gates in the high arched walls shut out the light from the street lamps. Only the glow in the evening sky above showed the piles of rubble and broken glass. A JCB digger stood gaunt and motionless, like the skeleton of the great dynosaur Miss Timmons had shown them in school.

Maura shivered. 'Let's give them their old ball back,' she said. 'It's spooky in here.'

'Scaredy cat!' jeered Imelda.

'I'm not scared,' said Maura. 'I'll hide if you can find some place to hide in.'

'In here, then!'

Maura looked in the direction May's voice had come from but May had disappeared. 'Where did she go?' she asked Imelda, but when she turned around Imelda had disappeared too. All she could hear was a sound like stones falling. She seemed to be in this awful place all by herself.

'Where are you?' she called.

'Sh! They'll hear you. We're over here.'

Maura peered into the darkness but she could see nothing. 'Where's "Here"?' she called, as softly as she could.

'In the hole.'

May's voice came from just in front of her. She moved cautiously forward. The demolition men had begun to excavate for the foundations of the new building that would soon rise up inside the old walls. May and Imelda had clambered down the side of the pit that had been dug and were crouched at the bottom.

Maura was scared. The pit was not very deep but she was still afraid she might slip and tear or dirty her clothes. Then she might have to tell where she had been. Either way, her mother would give out to her. Since her father had been out of work her mother often gave out to her.

On the other hand, if she showed she was scared May and Imelda might not let her play with them again. She was even more scared about that than about her mother giving out to her. Slowly, she edged her way down to join them.

Once she was down, she had to agree that it was a good place to hide. If they stood up, they could see everything between them and the gap in the hoarding where a shaft of light shone in from the street.

A shout from outside told the girls that the boys had spotted the gap in the hoarding. May put her finger to her lips and they all crouched even lower in the darkness.

'Bet ya they're in here.' It was Whacker's voice and the girls heard the sound of three bodies squeezing in through the gap.

'Come on out, May. We know you're there.' It was Richie this time. 'If you don't, we're comin' to get you.'

The girls froze, trying not to breathe as they heard the boys' footsteps blundering about above them.

'They mustn't be here!'

It was Whacker's voice again. May grinned. She heard the sound of feet running away. Then silence. She waited for what seemed like ages. Then she straightened up.

'There they are!' Whacker shouted behind her.

The boys were upon them now, with shouts of triumph, wresting the football out of May's arms.

'That's mean.' cried Imelda, 'Lettin' on to have gone like that.'

Whacker laughed. 'I knew ya'd fall for it. You're not nearly smart enough to beat us.'

'You'd never have found us if you hadn't tricked us,' May cried. 'But isn't this a great hiding place?'

'It's good all right,' agreed Richie, 'Do you know this place would be great for playin' Relieve-ee-o. There's loads and loads of space. Let's come tomorrow after tea.'

'Yeah, let's,' cried everyone except Maura. She

was still uneasy, wondering if they had been seen by anyone who might tell their parents where they'd been.

As they climbed back through the gap in the hoarding, she noticed a fat man standing beside a big black car on the other side of the road. He seemed to be watching them and when she glanced back he was still there, looking after them. He was a stranger and not likely to tell their parents what they had been doing. Yet there was something about his watchful stare that worried her. Why was he so interested in where they had been or where they were going?

2 Money on the Floor

After school the next day her mother sent May on a message to Macs. May loved going there because it had such a lovely smell – a mixture of oranges and fresh cakes.

Macs was near the corner of North King Street and Capel Street. There were shops nearer to the Square that sold the same things, but Mac would let you get things without paying for them, writing them down in a big red book. Then, at the end of the week, after May's father got paid, May would set off for Macs to pay off as much as possible of what was owing, with the money wrapped tightly in a screw of paper in her pocket.

The quickest way to Macs was down Green Street, past the old Court House. But often lately the streets around it had barricades across them, with little groups of policemen standing around, so May usually went down Ann Street, a narrow little road that she liked because it was called by a girl's name. She wondered who Ann was to have a street named after her. How nice it would be if someday there was a street named May Street after her!

When she had paid over the money and put the bread and milk in the string bag, she chose an orange iced lolly and set off down Capel Street.

May loved the bustle of Capel Street on a Friday evening. She always stopped outside the Pet Stores to peep in at the budgies in their cages and the puppies crawling around in the window. Then she would look up at the three golden balls of the pawnbrokers hanging against the sky as she walked underneath. Then she would push her way through the crowds hurrying in and out of the big hardware shop where Mickser's elder brother worked, selling nails and thumb tacks and curtain hooks.

Lower down the street, the pavements were crowded with men. Here there were pubs and bookmakers on every corner, and tobacconists and amusement arcades, loud with the noise of little steel balls banging off the sides of the pintables and the static hum of "The Space Invaders' machines.

This evening, as she turned the corner into Capel Street, she noticed a man standing outside the Public Library. She could not help noticing him because he was holding a book almost as big as himself. He was a small, crotchedy-looking little man, with a mean ferrety face, and his head jerked in little bird-like movements as he peered this way and that through the people and traffic hurrying past. He seemed to be looking for something.

Then a big black car, driven by a fat man with a red face, drew up at the side of the road.

'Where were ye?' snapped Ferrety Face. 'This thing's heavy.'

'I couldn't park here, could I?' The fat man

sounded sulky. Then he looked at the book. 'Could ya not have got something smaller?'

'All them books on archaeology are as big,' said Ferrety Face. 'Anyway this one shows the layout of the old monastic buildings.'

What the fat man said in reply, May could not hear, because by then Ferrety-Face had managed to heave the book on to the back seat and close the passenger door after him. The driver of a green van honked his horn at them twice. Mary guessed from the look on the ferrety face that his lips were moving in an answering curse. 'He's a nasty little man,' she thought. And what did those words 'archaeology' and 'monastic buildings' mean? 'Danny would know,' she decided, 'I must ask him after tea.'

But after tea, her mother told her to do her 'eckers', ready for school again on Monday. May had hoped to slip out without doing them. Now she raced through her sums for fear the others would go to the Markets without her. But they were still messing about in the Square, waiting for Whacker.

'He's helpin' Da fix the tap over the sink,' Imelda explained. Their father worked for the Corporation and Whacker never lost an opportunity to learn how to put in a new washer or unblock a sink. With so many out of work since the Markets moved, he knew the importance of learning a trade.

As soon as he arrived, they all set off for the gap in the hoarding. May had wondered whether Maura would come, remembering how scared she had been the evening before. But Maura was there, trudging along behind Imelda, her hands thrust deep into the pockets of her worn gaberdine. They went straight to where the girls had been hiding on the previous evening.

'Janey!' gasped May as she reached the hole and stood teetering on the edge. 'They've made it a lot bigger.'

'Yeah, and a lot deeper,' agreed Mickser. 'They musta had the digger at it agin today.'

With his left foot, Richie tested a small ledge of stone that stuck out at one side of the hole.

'I'm gonna go down into it,' he said. The others watched as he lowered himself into the hole.

'I bet there's a snake down there!' called May. 'It's gonna come out of a crack and get ye!'

'You'd better keep your mouth shut or you'll swally it,' yelled Mickser.

'Like Johnny,' laughed Imelda. She and May started to clap hands together, singing,

> *Johnny gave me apples, Johnny gave me pears,*
> *Johnny gave me sixpence to kiss him on the stairs,*
> *I gave him back his apples, I gave him back his pears,*
> *I gave him back his sixpence and flung him down the*
>   *stairs.*
> *He jumped in the lake and he swallied a snake,*
> *And he came back up with a belly-ache!*

'Yez'll have more than a belly-ache if ye don't get out of here in double-quick time,' snarled a threatening voice. They swung round to see two men coming towards them. They were wearing dark overcoats and they looked very angry.

Automatically the gang scattered, running in different directions, but the two men made no attempt to chase them as they slipped back through the hoarding.

Once outside they held a council of war behind a parked car.

'Did you see that fat man with the long black bag?' panted Maura. 'Well, I seen him yesterday when we were leaving the Markets. He was standin' beside a big black car over there.'

'And I seen him this evening in Capel Street', May added excitedly, 'The other man with the ferrety face was with him. Fatser was driving the car and Ferrety-Face was gettin' in. With a big book.' Then she remembered something.

'Richie's still down the hole'.

'Oh, what'll they do to him?' wailed Maura.

'They can't do a thing,' said Whacker. 'They're not builder's men. Not with a big black car and dressed the way they were. We have as much right there as they have. Let's go back in.'

The words were hardly out of his mouth when a mop of red hair appeared in the gap, followed by Richie's head and body. He was hoarse with excitement.

'Those fellas are up to something!' he said. 'I vote we find out what!'

'What did they say to you?' asked May.

'Nothing,' Richie grinned. 'They didn't see me. They were too busy with the yoke.'

'The yoke?'

'Whatever it is they had in the long black bag. As soon as you'd gone, they took it out and the next thing they were fightin' over what way to put it together.'

'What did it look like?' asked Whacker.

'I dunno,' said Richie. 'The minute they started arguing I slipped out. Let's take a decko.'

The others followed him back to the hoarding. The gap was only big enough for two to look in at the same time, one above the other. Richie and Whacker got there first and peeped in cautiously. At first, looking into the dark interior, nothing was visible. But as their eyes got used to the darkness, they could see Fatser moving backwards and forwards, holding something in his hand that looked like a vacuum cleaner.

Suddenly, Whacker turned from the hole, his eyes ablaze.

'I know what they're at!' he whispered. 'That thing they're using is a metal detector. Ya can find money with it. I seen one just like it on the telly. And the man said the fella holdin' it had found a whole lot of old coins on a farm somewhere in England. Roman coins. They showed us the farm an' all. And the hole in the ground where they dug up the money.'

'Then them two must be lookin' for money,' cried Richie. 'No wonder they don't want us around.'

He ran back to look through the gap. Fatser was working systematically up and down the space from right to left, listening carefully on his earphones for the slightest change in the whirring noise that came from the detector.

Suddenly Richie felt a wet tongue on his arm. His dog, Patchie, was standing beside him.

'Go home, Patchie,' he whispered. But Patchie just wagged his tail at his master. He didn't want to go home. Suddenly he stiffened. The rough hair on the back of his neck stood up like the hairs on a shaving brush. He had got the scent of the two men and he didn't like what he smelt. The little mongrel began to quiver as a growl started deep inside him.

'Quiet,' warned Richie, trying to muzzle the dog's mouth, but it was too late. The low rumbling sound grew into an angry growl. Excited as the two men were, they heard it and looked up. The gang jumped back from the gap, but they had been spotted.

'Get away from here, ya little devils.' shouted Fatser. He lumbered to the gap and stuck his head out. But the gang had scattered and all he could see was a small white dog with one black ear and a black patch on his side, growling at him.

'Just wait 'til I lay my hands on you kids,' Fatser shouted. From the way he spread his fat sausage-like fingers it was clear that he longed to squeeze them around someone's throat.

After a minute, he pulled his head in again and the gang cautiously edged back towards the hoarding.

Greatly daring, Maura peeped in through the bottom of the gap. She could see Fatser unplugging the arm of the metal detector and putting the cover over the search head. 'We can do nothing while they're around', she heard Ferrety-Face grumble. Fatser nodded. He slipped off the earphones, unbuckled the belt and put all the equipment into the black nylon carry-bag. In a few minutes there was the sound of a gate opening and closing.

'They're goin'!' Maura whispered to May, 'They musta got in the way the builders do.'

The gang took cover behind a parked lorry as a sleek black car turned the corner and drove off towards Church Street. As the car disappeared, they straightened up. Whacker let out a whistle.

'A Mercedes 200! They must have pots of money.'

'They didn't find anything,' said Imelda.

'That means they'll be back,' said Richie, 'We've no time to lose. We have to start right now.'

Maura's eyes grew big and round. 'You mean, we're gonna look for the money?'

'What else?' Richie grinned. 'We know it's in there somewhere. All we have to do is find it! But we need a pick and shovel.'

'Could you get the lend of a loan of one offa the

Corpo?' suggested Mickser to Whacker.

Whacker shook his head. 'They'll have them all locked up at this time of night, an' tomorrow may be too late. We'll have to use anything we can get.'

'There's the fire-irons in our parlour,' May said.

'I'll see if I can get something outa Da's tool box,' said Whacker.

'We'll want a flash lamp,' Richie said.

'I could maybe get the lamp offa me Da's bike.' 'An' me Ma has a torch she uses when she gets the turf outa the back at night.' Mickser and Imelda spoke together.

'Right.' Richie spoke urgently now. 'Go and get what you can. And hurry! I'll keep cavey . . . in case Fatser and Ferrety-Face come back. And take Patchie back, May. We don't want him giving us away again.'

But in spite of whistles and pushes, Patchie refused to budge. He sat down firmly on the curb at Richie's side, almost as if he was guarding him against something. Suddenly May remembered the skipping rope she always carried. She tied it around Patchie's neck and gave it a twitch. With a sad look at Richie, Patchie allowed himself to be dragged back to the Square.

When May reached home she could hear the telly going in the front parlour. She pushed open the door and peeped in. Her father was there on his own, watching the greyhound racing. She began to creep round the back of the chair, keeping one eye on her father's head. His chair was sideways to the fireplace. If she did not make a sound, she might be able to grab the fire-irons and slip out again. But they would not be easy to grab without making a noise.

There was a poker, a shovel and a tongs, all shining brightly, for her mother somehow found the time to polish them every day. It occurred to her that the tongs would not be much use in digging for buried treasure. But could she lift the shovel and poker off their hooks without making them rattle?

She took a last peep at the back of her father's head and then made a grab for the two fire-irons. She lifted them clear of the stand but, as she turned to slip out, she caught the side of the tongs with the shovel and it swung against the stand with a tell-tale clank.

'What are ya at there?' called her father.

May froze but he never took his eyes from the screen. 'Just gettin' something Da,' she said, hiding her booty under her coat.

'No call to be making such a clatter over it,' muttered her father, but she was already half-way to Mary's Abbey.

Glancing back, she saw Mickser racing after her. He was carrying a large bicycle lamp. Then halfway up Michan's Street they overtook Imelda who had a small hand torch. But when they got to Mary's Lane there was no sign of either Maura or Whacker. Worse, there was no sign of Richie either!

He was not at the gap in the hoarding nor hiding behind any of the cars in the Lane.

'Supposin' Fatser and Ferrety-Face came back and got him?' whispered Imelda.

'Richie wouldn't be got that easy!' said May loyally, but she suddenly felt the night air chill on her cheek and shivered a little. Then she heard a sound from the other side of the hoarding.

'He's inside,' she cried in relief and, climbing in through the gap, ran straight into the arms of Fatser. Behind Fatser was Ferrety-Face, holding Richie tightly by the arms.

3 Three Chips in the Pan

'Listen, you kids,' said Fatser, 'Yez gotta stop this trespassing, d'ya hear me?. This place isn't a playground. Yez could fall into one of the holes and break yer leg.'

He was trying to sound as if he cared whether they broke a leg or not, May thought, but he wasn't really very good at it. 'Do you own the place?' she asked cheekily.

'Of course we do,' blustered Fatser. 'And if we have any more trouble with you lot we'll hand yez over to the police. They'll put manners on ya '

'And if they don't, I will,' muttered Ferrety-Face, and, though he was smaller than Fatser, May somehow felt more scared of him.

'Now, get out the pair of yez,' said Fatser, pushing her towards the gap in the hoarding. 'And take care I don't set eyes on yez again, or yez'll be sorry.'

Richie and May squeezed back out on to the street, almost colliding with Mickser and Imelda. They didn't say a word until they were safely back in the Square.

'How did they catch ye?' asked Imelda.

'They must have only been lettin' on to go, so as to fool us,' said Richie, 'cos you were only gone when they were back. I was tryin' to see what they were up to when I got this desperate tickle in my nose. I put my finger under it to try to hold back the sneeze only it didn't work. I let out a right good one and the two of them was on me in a flash. I couldn't warn you because old Ferrety-Face had his hand over my mouth.'

'The mean things,' May was raging. 'Now they'll get all the money for themselves.'

'Maybe they won't be able to find it,' said Mickser without too much conviction.

'Of course, they'll find it! Haven't they got that old metal detector?'

At that moment, they saw Whacker's sturdy figure moving towards them and they made room for him in the little circle of light under the street lamp.

'What kept ye?' asked Richie.

'Getting this,' said Whacker, holding up a heavy claw-hammer. 'My Dad was around and I had to get him outa the way. But I thought we were to meet at the Markets. I ducked out the back way.'

They told him all that had happened. But he had even more to tell them.

'It was only luck I didn't run clean into them two myself. I was just turnin' the corner when Ferrety-Face stuck his head out through the gap in the hoarding. Then a squad car came cruisin' by and he ducked back in again real fast. I hid behind a car and waited. After a bit, Ferrety Face took a decko up and down the street. Then the pair of them piled into the Merc with all their gear and hit out in a hurry.'

May's face was alight with triumph. 'They mustn't have found the money so, after they chased us away. There wasn't time!'

Richie agreed. 'Then we'll have another go tomorrow. Meet here after dinner and bring any more tools you can get.'

'Will I tell Maura?' asked May.

'I dunno,' said Richie. 'What happened her that she didn't turn up tonight?'

'She was scared,' Imelda said, 'I knew she wouldn't come back.'

'Then leave her out of it,' Richie decided.

The next day, being Saturday, May had to mind the baby for her mother. She wheeled him out into the Square in his go-cart and played games with him like *Clap Hands till Dadda Comes Home* and *One Potato, Two Potato,* while at the same time she kept an eye on her two younger brothers.

Imelda had no baby brother or sister but she borrowed Mrs. Doyle's baby from the south side of the Square. With four children under the age of six and no older girl to mind them for her, Mrs. Doyle was always glad to have Imelda borrow her Billy. The two girls pushed the go-carts around the Square side by side, grumbling the way they heard their mothers do.

'Go on now and have a little play for yerself,'

Imelda would scold one of the Doyle toddlers, 'and don't be gettin' under my feet all morning.' And she would turn to May, saying, 'That young wan's like a bag of cats today. You can't look crooked at her or she'll whinge.'

May would nod sympathetically. 'Don't I know? Mine are the very same. That Brendan's after my heels all day. I can't stir for him.'

But in spite of their words the girls looked forward to their weekly half-day of motherhood. It made them feel very grown-up while at the same time enjoying the childish games as much as the babies. They got a kick out of the infants' chortles when they were tickled at the end of *Round and Round the Garden,* and it was nice to hear the laughter of the young Doyles and Byrnes playing *Paddy on the Railway* or *Yip, Yip, a Nanny Goat.*

But this Saturday they felt as if the morning would never end. Their minds were full of their plans for the afternoon. Was there really money buried under the floor and, if so, could they possibly find it and get it safely away before Fatser and Ferrety-Face came back?

When Maura crossed the Square on the way to the shops on a message for her mother, May and Imelda pretended to be so busy that they did not see her. Maura stared miserably at them. She supposed they were black out with her for not going back to the meeting place the night before. How could she explain that it hadn't been just because she was afraid, but also because of the way her mother had carried on when she caught her sneaking out of the house. It was awful at home since the Markets had moved from Mary's Abbey, with her mother all the time nagging her father about spending the money he got from the Labour on drink and cigarettes. She knew she would have to wait till she had a chance to do something for May or Imelda and then maybe they would be spin spout again.

As soon as Maura was out of earshot, the two girls started to talk again.

'Why would anyone want to bury money under the Markets?' Imelda asked. 'It makes no sense.'

It was then May remembered Danny's story about the old Abbey.

'Maybe it was buried there before the Markets were built. When the old Abbey was there. Danny said parts of the Abbey may still be there, under the ground.'

'But how would Fatser and Ferrety-Face know that?'

May thought about it. And then it came to her! Danny knew everything because of all the books he had read. When she had seen Fatser and Ferrety-Face in Capel Street, they had just taken a huge book out of the Public Library.

She jumped to her feet. 'Come on, let's go across and ask Danny.'

When Danny opened the door he smiled at the sight of the two girls with their babies.

36

'Well, well, what can I do for the two of ye this morning?' he asked.

'We wanted to ask you something, Danny,' said May.

'It's about a book,' said Imelda.

'It's not exactly one book,' May corrected. 'It's a whole lot of books that are all together in one part of the Library. They're about archaeology. What does 'archaeology' mean?'

'It's studying the way things used to be,' said Danny, 'Like over at Wood Quay.'

'You mean, diggin' things up?' May cried in excitement.

Danny nodded again, 'That's part of it, right enough.'

'Would diggin' up ould coins be archaeology?'

'Certainly it would. Coins, old bones, anything from the past.'

The two girls jumped up and down, hugging each other like footballers who have scored a goal.

'Then that's it!' cried Imelda. 'That's how they knew.'

'How who knew what?' asked Danny.

'It's a secret, Danny,' May said regretfully. She would have loved to tell him all about it but she knew Richie would be angry if she did.

'Ah well, of course, that's different,' said Danny. 'You must never tell a secret.'

'One thing more, Danny,' said May, 'What's a "monastic building"?'

'It's a monastery, of course. Like Mary's Abbey.'

'Thank you, Danny,' said May solemnly. 'I'm sorry I can't tell you anything about it now, but I promise when I can tell, I'll tell you first.'

'Fair enough!' said Danny. 'Wait now till I see can I find ye a biscuit.'

While Danny went off to rummage in the kitchen in the old tin with the picture of a sailing ship on the lid, Imelda turned to May.

' Ya never said about the monastic building.'

'I only just remembered it. Ferrety-Face said he got the book because it showed the lay-out of the old monastic building.'

'Then it's for definite,' said Imelda. 'They know there's money buried there.'

'I hope I can get the fire-irons again,' May was worried. She had had to slip them back again before she went to bed. Her mother always gave them a special rub on a Saturday morning. There was no chance she would not notice they were missing. She would have to get them again somehow. Imelda, on the other hand, had her contribution tucked away in the go-car. It was the bucket and spade she had had since the time she went to Dollymount Strand on the parish outing two years ago. May secretly thought they would be even less use than her fire-irons, but it was hard to get real tools.

When they finally assembled, Mickser had brought the most impressive contribution. It was a garden fork his father had somehow acquired while doing nixers as a gardener for the well-to-do up around the North Circular Road.

Richie was the last to arrive. Since their father worked for the Post Office, May could not imagine any tools coming from that source. But Richie carried a strange-looking object.

Whacker eyed it dubiously. 'What d'ya call that, Redser?' he asked.

Richie grinned. 'It's a class of a pick.'

'Made it yerself, did ye?' enquired Mickser.

Richie nodded. 'I picked up the broken anchor last week on the dump, so all I had to do was fix it on the brush handle.'

'Show it here to me.' Whacker held out an expert hand. He took the strange object and swung it. Then he nodded. 'It oughta hold for a while anyway,' he said. 'And it's not as heavy as it looks.'

The little group set off for the buildings, trying to keep their strange collection of tools as much out of sight as possible. They approached the gap in the hoarding cautiously, but there was nothing inside now but a pair of pigeons, bustling about and pecking at the ground.

'Lookin' for buried treasure too.' giggled Imelda.

The place looked quite different now, with sunshine pouring in where the roof used to be, and the shivery feeling of last evening left them. It was all just a game again.

'Let's start in one of the holes,' said Mickser, 'The concrete's already bust up there and we've only the one pick for bustin' more:'

'Good thinkin',' said Whacker. 'Pick a hole.'

Imelda began pointing to each hole in turn, as if she were picking sides for Relieve-ee-O, chanting·

> *Eena, mena, tippy, teena,*
> *A baa, booshalom,*
> *X, Y. Number Nine,*
> *Out goes you!*
> *Out goes one,*
> *Out goes two,*
> *Out goes the little girl,*
> *Dressed in blue ...*

'That's stupid!' said Richie. 'Let's start here.'

Mickser went over and threw a lump of broken concrete down into the pit. They could all hear the splash.

'It rained last night,' Whacker said. 'That won't make diggin' easier.'

'We can bale it out with my bucket,' said Imelda.

Richie was already clambering down into the hole. It was the one he had hidden in the day before so he already knew the best footholds. After he had baled out the water with Imelda's bucket, they all got into the hole. Whacker gouged out stones with his claw-hammer, Richie prised up slabs with the poker, while Mickser loosened the ground in the middle with the fork. May and Imelda shovelled it away with the spade and the fire shovel. They worked hard and in silence.

Then May said, 'It's gonna take ages and ages to dig all of it.'

The others rested their aching backs and looked around. Nobody wanted to agree with her, but when they looked at the huge space all around them and then back to the ground they had dug, they knew she was right. They would never do it without Fatser's metal detector to tell them the right place to dig.

'We can't give up now,' said Richie. 'Let's give it another ten minutes.'

'How will we know ten minutes is up?' asked May, 'We have no watch.'

'I know,' said Whacker. 'We'll make a timer. I seen them do it on the telly.' Even though they all felt a bit down, the others smiled. Everything worth seeing, Whacker had seen on the telly.

He fetched a bit of cardboard from near the gate and twisted it into a funnel, like an ice-cream cone. Then he filled it with sand from the pile dumped in one corner. He propped it against a ledge at the side of the hole, took a pin from behind the lapel of his jacket and pierced a small hole in the bottom. The sand began to trickle slowly out of the hole.

'When the cone is empty,' said Whacker, 'we'll stop.'

'The sand's comin' out real slow,' said May, peering at Whacker's timer, 'an' it's tricklin' down past the three funny little chips in the stone.'

'You mean, on the pan!' said Imelda and began
to chant:

> *Three chips on the pan,*
> *Three chips on the pan,*
> *Turn them over, turn them over,*
> *Three chips on the pan.*

'Are yous two gonna stop messin' and shovel or
not?' demanded Richie from below.'

'As soon as I've turned the chips over,' said May
giggling, and she put her hand to the ledge. There
was a sudden loud rumbling sound. Whacker's
timer was sent sent spinning into space.

May cried out in surprise and the others all
turned to look. There, where the shelf of rock had
been, was a rectangular hole, like a small press with
the door open. And inside the press was a large,
dirt-blackened box.

'What did I do?' asked May startled.

Whacker gave a sort of a whoop. ' Ya found the
treasure, that's what ya done!' he shouted. 'I bet
you that tin is stuffed full of old coins that are worth
millions.'

4 *Turn them over, Turn them over*

Everyone crowded round the edge of the hole, gazing at the box sitting on its little shelf in the rock. It was covered with dust and cobwebs.

'It musta been there for years!' whispered Richie, hardly daring to breathe.

'And we'd never have found it only Imelda and me were singing that old skippin' song,' said May.

'It's like followin' a clue in a treasure hunt,' said Imelda. ' "Jelly on the plate" must be the clue to where it was hid.'

'That's stupid,' said Mickser. 'And, anyway, it doesn't say "three chips on the stone". It says "three chips on the pan". It means chips you fry, not chips you make with a chisel.'

'All the same, it says, "Turn them over, turn them over" and that's how I found it.' said May.

'Never mind how ya found it. Let's see what's in it.' said Whacker.

But that was easier said than done. The box was so heavy it took three of them to lift it out and, when they had done so, they found it was locked.

Whacker fetched his hammer and began trying to prise the lock open with the claws, but it was so crusted with rust that he could get no proper grip.

The others could not bear to wait any longer.

'Break it open, can't you?' shouted Mickser.

'Hit it a bash with the hammer!' yelled Richie.

'It's a shame to smash up the box,' said May. 'Look at the funny drawings on it – like birds in a circle. It's awful pretty.'

'It's so dirty you can hardly see,' said Mickser, 'Besides what's inside may be a lot prettier. Whacking big gold coins or something!'

Whacker looked from one to the other 'Well,' he asked, 'Am I to smash the box or not?'

'Yes!' cried Mickser and Richie and Imelda.

'No!' cried May.

'One against four.' Whacker said. 'Stand back.'

He brought the heavy hammer down on top of the lock with a crash and the lid flew open. All the heads bent over it at once, so that they banged in the middle. But inside the box was only a strange, dark piece of material. Whacker touched it.

'It's leather,' he said, 'that's gone funny.'

He lifted a piece of leather and underneath it there was another box. This one still gleamed a little here and there where the leather had protected it.

'This one's even prettier,' said May, 'It's shaped like a little house. And look at the ends of the roof! They're like animals' heads with their mouths open.'

'It's still only an ould box!' said Mickser. 'A box inside another box. Suppose there's only another box inside that!'

'We'll soon find out,' said Whacker trying it, but the second box was locked too.

'Can't you open it the way you opened the other one?' Mickser cried impatiently.

'You can't smash the little house,' protested May.

Suddenly they heard voices outside. They all froze. They had been so excited over their find, they had forgotten Fatser and Ferrety-Face. Richie crept to the gap in the hoarding and peeped out. After a second he returned.

'It was only old Baldy Conscience from the pawnshop.'

They all breathed a sigh of relief.

'All the same,' said Richie, 'Fatser and Ferrety-Face could be back soon. Let's take the box back to the Square.'

'What will we do with the first box?' asked Imelda, looking at the dirty black box with its lid all askew.

'Leave it there!' said Mickser. 'It's no good.'

Richie shook his head. 'The minute Fatser and Ferrety-Face saw it they'd know we'd got here ahead of them and then they'd come after us.'

'They'll know anyway,' said Whacker, 'Just as soon as they see the little shelf at the side of the hole.'

'Maybe it will close again.' said May. She turned the stone with the three chips on it back the way it had been in the first place. With a rumble, the slab came down again, shutting off the little shelf, so that no one would ever guess that it was there. They all cheered.

'Sh!' said Richie. 'Them two could be outside in the street. See can you open it again, May?'

Once again May turned the stone and once again the slab moved to reveal the little space.

'I've an idea,' said Richie. 'See if you can get the first box to close, Whacker.'

Whacker fiddled with it but the lid would not stay down. 'I could hammer the top so it would hold.'

'Then we'll fill it with bits of cement and stones 'til it's real heavy again.' said Richie.

'Great!' said Whacker laughing. 'And then we hammer the lid down and put it back on the shelf the way it was. I'd like to see Fatser's face when they open it.'

It did not take long to fill the box with rubble and to hammer the lid on again. Then they put it back on the shelf. It was no longer covered in dust and cobwebs and the lid showed the marks of Whacker's hammer.

'It doesn't really look the same,' cried May.

'Can't be helped,' said Richie, 'Let's get back to the Square and open the box.'

When they got back to the Square they found that the lock on the little box shaped like a house was hardly rusted at all. Even Mickser agreed that it would be a shame to smash it open. So Whacker prised it gently with is pen-knife. When it finally yielded, they all cried out in disappointment.

The box was not full of gold coins. There was no money in it at all. Only the same dark clammy material that Whacker had said was leather 'gone funny'. Inside the leather there was an old pot and a plate, made of dull, dirty-looking metal.

'It's not the treasure at all,' said Mickser in disgust. 'Only a stupid old pot.'

'Wouldn't it sicken ye?' said Imelda. 'After all the diggin' we done.'

'Ye mean, after all the diggin' Richie and Mickser and me done' said her brother. 'Yez only shovelled the dirt outa the way.'

'Are we gonna go on lookin' for the treasure?' asked May.

'Of course.' said Richie, sounding indecisive. 'Tomorrow, maybe.'

'Richie! May! Will yez come in to your tea!'

It was their mother calling from the other side of the Square. For once they were glad of the excuse to go.

'What are we gonna do with these?' asked Whacker, pushing at the dirty-looking pot with his foot. 'We can't leave them here. Someone might want to know where we got them.'

Richie shrugged. It did not seem to matter now.

An excited yapping made them all turn to look towards the middle of the Square. All they could see was Patchie's back legs and stumpy tail. The rest of

him was buried in the hole he was digging as if his life depended on it.

'Oh Patchie!' cried May, 'You bold boy!'

Patchie took no notice. His back legs quivered with excitement as he dug deeper and deeper into the grass patch, making excited little noises like he sometimes did in his sleep. Suddenly he stopped and started to back up and out of the hole, his tail wagging so that his whole backside shook. He was so covered in mud that he looked more like a completely black dog than a white one with one black patch. In his mouth was an ancient bone.

'He must be an archaeological dog,' said May, not knowing whether to laugh or to cry.''cos he's diggin' up old bones.'

'He's made an awful mess of the grass,' said Imelda. 'Danny won't like that.'

May nodded. 'We'll only have to fill up the hole again and wait for the grass to grow back.'

'Hey!' said Mickser, 'Why don't we stick the pot down the hole before we fill it in? It'll be safe here and no one will know that we have it.'

The pot and the plate fitted perfectly into the hole. When the clay had been shovelled on top of the box, Mickser cut out a sod with the grass growing on it and put it over the top of the filled-in hole. Then he stamped on it. They all examined it critically.

'A blind man on a gallopin' horse would never see it,' said Imelda.

'Will ye be out after tea?' asked Mickser. Richie nodded.

There was another shout of 'Richie! May!', and the two of them ran across the Square. As they opened the door, Patchie bounded in after them, carrying his bone.

'Will yez get that dirty animal outa here!' cried their mother looking with horror at his muddy footprints all over her clean hallway. Patchie lay down in front of the kitchen cooker gnawing his bone.

'Can he not stop where he is?' pleaded May. 'He'll not stir now that he has the bone. And I'll give him a bath directly after the tea.'

'Well, keep an eye on him then,' said her mother crossly as she set the heavy teapot down on the table.

'He's a real heart scald, that dog of yours.'

But May knew that for all her rough words her mother would never hurt Patchie nor leave him short of food as long as they had a bite to eat themselves.

She and Richie both had great appetites after all their hard work and they ate their way through half the large sliced pan.

'Thanks be to God I've a steady job,' said their father as he put on his jacket before going out to join his mates in the pub on the Quays. 'That pair'd eat you out of house and home. There's no filling them.'

After the tea, May filled the bowl her mother

used for boiling clothes and gave Patchie his bath. 'I won't let him out for a while,' she told her mother. 'Not until he's quite dry.'

It was while May was sweeping out the hall that there was a knock on the road. It was Mrs. Doyle.

'Is Richie in?' she asked.

'Yes, he's watching the telly.' said May.

'I want him to do a message for me. I'm after plugging in the iron and fusing all the lights and the young wan's screaming her head off. Mr. Doyle's down in Flynn's and I daren't leave the childer while I run down after him.'

As Richie, dragged away from his western, set out for Flynn's Public House, Patchie suddenly leapt to his feet and shot out of the door after him.

'Come back this minute!' shouted May, but Patchie pretended not to hear her and trotted along at Richie's heels as if he were the most obedient dog in the world.

Half way across the Square, they met Whacker.

'I thought ya were never coming out,' he said. 'Did you forget or what?'

'I was watchin' the fillum,' Richie told him, 'Now I've to run down to Flynns for Mrs. Doyle.'

'I'll come with ya ,' Whacker offered. 'Mickser didn't show either.'

Richie nodded. 'He was fed up over not findin' the money.'

'Me too. But we are gonna go on lookin', aren't we?'

'I dunno. It could be anywhere. We don't know where to start without a metal detector.'

'But we can't leave it for Fatser and Ferrety-Face to find. I bet they're there this minute lookin'. For all we know they could have found where to dig by now.'

They cut into the dark narrow street that led to the Quays.

'I suppose the two of us could take a decko after we've seen Mr. Doyle,' suggested Richie. 'At least then we'd know if … '

But he never finished the sentence. Suddenly, from one of the dark doorways ahead of them, two figures sprang out. Before the boys could turn and run they found themselves enveloped in the thick folds of two potato sacks. They struggled but they had been taken so completely by surprise that they were powerless to prevent themselves from being slung over the men's shoulders like the sacks of potatoes they appeared to be. The next minute they found themselves being slung on to a hard floor and heard a van door being slammed shut behind them.

They were prisoners! And it would be hours before anyone in the Square began to wonder what had happened to them.

5 *Wibbly-wobbly, Wibbly-wobbly*

Richie lay still in the back of the van, bracing his feet against the side to try to stop himself from rolling about. He had already discovered that any movement inside the sack made it harder to breathe. Besides, he was listening, Since he could see nothing, feeling and hearing were the only ways of telling where they were going.

They must be heading towards the Phoenix Park. He was nearly sure of that, because he would have felt it if the van had swung to the right or the left out of the one-way flow of traffic on the north side of the river. He had often been up to the Park to give Patchie a run or play football or look for the deer. Once they had even been to the Zoo.

Now they were stopping. The traffic lights must be against them. It could not be the ones near their own corner on the city side of the Four Courts. They had already gone too far for that. It was probably the one at the corner of Church Street, where Danny had told them the first bridge over the Liffey had been built

Suddenly Richie heard barking. It was faint to begin with but it kept getting louder until he was certain that he knew that high-pitched bark. It was Patchie.

Richie's heart began to thump with excitement. Good old Patchie! He was following the van.

The van kept going without turning either to the right or to the left. Once or twice it stopped again at traffic lights, but, although Richie strained his ears for the sound of distant barking over the roar of the traffic, he did not hear it again.

'He's still somewhere there,' he told himself. 'He's just saving his breath for running. He only barked before to let me know he was followin'.' But he did not really believe this. Patchie could not keep up with a van unless the traffic was moving really slowly.

Then Richie heard the sound of a train somewhere over to the left. The train was slowing, almost stopping. It must be pulling into Heuston Station. So they were going to the Phoenix Park after all!

Suddenly, Richie found himself slithering across the floor, bumping into Whacker. The van was turning left. They must be crossing the Liffey then, going towards Kilmainham, not towards the Park. He braced his feet again, thinking about Kilmainham. He and Whacker had gone with the school to Kilmainham Gaol one day to see the yard where Connolly had been shot in a chair and the little cell that had once held de Valera. Now they were prisoners too, like them.

Before Richie had found a proper grip with his feet he was slithering back the other way. The van was turning right. Then it stopped. After a few moments, he heard the creak of a gate opening. The van moved forward a little. Then it stopped once more. Ferrety-Face must have got out to open a gate. Now Fatser was waiting for him.

The gate creaked again, this time behind them. The van started to move forward once more. Now the ground was bumpy under the wheels. Richie was buffeted about on the hard floor, banging his head against something sharp in the back. He felt bruised and sick, and he could no longer hear the sound of traffic. Wherever could they be?

Suddenly the van pulled up with a jerk. Richie became aware of a strange roaring sound that he could not identify. Next thing the back door of the van was being slid open. He could feel a cold wind blowing through the sacking over his head. He was grabbed and dragged from the van.

When the sack was pulled from his head, Richie could not believe his eyes. All around him were great stone pillars and strange machinery. The machinery was like nothing he had ever seen before. It was big and black and cumbersome and all cogs and wheels. And all around was the strange rushing, roaring sound he had heard the minute the van had stopped. He started to shout for help. Whacker shouted too.

Ferrety-Face gave Richie's arm a vicious little twist.

'Yez can shout 'til your lungs burst,' he said. 'Yez

will not be heard over the noise of the weir.'

So that was what caused the roaring sound; water plunging over a weir and echoing through this big, cold, cavernous building. But what sort of a building was it, open to the river that rushed past on one side? Then it dawned on Richie what all that huge, old-fashioned machinery really was. Those cogs and wheels had once been part of an old mill that had ground flour for baking and maize for chick-mash and all the other things that to-day were done by modern, oil-driven machinery. He and Whacker were in an old, ruined mill!

Ferrety-Face pushed Richie against one of the rough stone pillars. Then he picked up a piece of rope and tied him tightly to the pillar.

Richie kicked out sideways and got Ferrety-Face in the shins. Ferrety-Face cursed and hit him across the face. 'Try that again and ye 'll be sorry,' he said.

'It's yez'll be sorry when my Da catches yez ,' Richie heard Whacker say, but the two men only laughed.

'He'll have to find us first, won't he?' said Fatser.

Richie managed to turn his head and saw that Whacker was tied to the pillar beside him. He twisted back to look at Ferrety-Face. 'What do yez want from us anyway?' he demanded.

'What do ya think?' snarled Ferrety-Face. 'We want what yez took outa the ould Abbey. An' yez better hand it over quick.'

'But we never found the treasure,' Richie cried.

'There's no good telling lies,' said Fatser. 'We found the box yez forced open.'

'An' had the neck to stuff full of rocks,' Ferrety-Face growled angrily. 'Yez deserve to be taught a lesson. I'd enjoy giving it to yez!'

Richie shivered. There was something about that mean little face that suggested that he was not joking.

'But there was nothin' in the box only rubbish,' said Whacker. 'There was no treasure there at all.'

Ferrety-Face picked up another piece of rope and said: 'Maybe this'll make yez change your mind.'

'But we're tellin' you the truth. Honest we are,' said Richie. 'I swear we haven't got the treasure.'

Ferrety-Face came towards them, swinging the piece of rope menacingly.

'Hang on there a minute,' Fatser said, 'A few hours by themselves in this place may do more than a beating. Besides I'm hungry. Let's go down to the gatehouse and get something to eat. We'll come back after midnight. Them two will feel differently then, after all that time in the cold and the dark with no food. They'll tell the truth then, I'll bet. But if not, ya can go to work on them with the rope.'

Ferrety-Face seemed disappointed. Then Fatser continued: 'There's a bottle or two to go with the food.'

Ferrety-Face brightened a little at that. 'Right.' he said. Then he laughed nastily. 'And these two buckoos needn't mind about the cold. I'll warm them up when I get back.'

With that the two of them left, the sound of their footsteps echoing through the old stone building. Then Whacker and Richie heard the sound of the van starting up and driving away. They were all alone in the ruined mill.

'Next time keep yer bright ideas to yerself!' said Whacker. 'If we hadn't filled that ould box with stones and put it back we wouldn't be in this trouble. We shoulda taken it with us. Then they'd nevera known we found it.'

'He's probably right at that,' Richie thought ruefully. Aloud he said: 'I wouldn'ta minded but we got no treasure either. Whata we gonna do Whacker?'

'I dunno,' said Whacker. 'We're in right trouble this time. It's bad enough to be beaten for not tellin' something you do know. But now it looks as though we're gonna get bet for not tellin' somethin' we don't know.'

'An' as long as we don't tell them they'll go on beatin' us,' said Richie. 'An' it won't be like one of the Da's beatings either. I don't like the way that Ferrety-Face looks when he even thinks about it.'

'We'll have to make up a yarn,' said Whacker.

'That's not gonna work with that pair,' said Richie. 'They won't let us out of this 'til we hand over the treasure, and we can't hand over what we haven't got.'

'Supposin' we say it's at home?' suggested Whacker. 'If they once set foot in the Square, we'd have them.'

'They're too well up to be taken that easy.'

'So what do we do instead?' asked Whacker.

'I dunno. But they're not gonna be easy to fool.'

'We gotta think of something,' said Whacker.

There was silence then for a long time, except for the sound of the river rushing by before plunging down over the weir. Their arms were hurting from the ropes that bound them tightly to the damp pillars. Richie could feel ice cold drips on his arms as moisture trickled down them. 'The pillars are all wet,' he said. 'We'll get our death of cold. Did you think of anythin' yet?'

'Only that I'm awful hungry,' said Whacker. 'Maybe the others will come lookin' for us.'

'They wouldn't know where to look,' Richie said. 'I never even knew this place was here.'

'Where exactly are we anyway?' Whacker asked.

'In an ould mill at Islandbridge,' Richie told him. 'We turned off the bridge somehow before we was even half-ways across it.'

'Listen to X-Ray Eyes,' said Whacker. 'Very interestin', I'm sure, but not a lot of help.'

'I wish that ould black hook hangin' over there was a bit nearer,' said Richie. 'The edge on it still looks sharp. If I could only reach it to rub the rope against it, it might cut it!'

'An' if we had some jam we could have bread and

jam, if we had any bread,' said Whacker. 'Ya'd want to do a bit better than that, Redser me boy. Them two'll be back soon.'

'It looks bad,' Richie agreed.

'It looks very bad,' Whacker answered. 'But keep yer good side up. We're not dead yet!' He began to whistle *O'Donnell Abu*, the bravest and most warlike tune that he knew.

After a minute or two, Richie joined in. The sound bounced off the mill walls and became like the noise of a band of men on the march. This made Richie and Whacker feel much better so they kept on whistling. Suddenly they heard a familiar bark.

'Hurray!' said Richie. 'It's Patchie. He heard us whistlin'!'

'Good ould Patchie,' cried Whacker, as a ball of white fur hurled itself against Richie, its stump of a tail wagging wildly. 'How did he find us?'

'He followed the van,' said Richie. 'I heard him when we were drivin' up the Quays. But then I thought he'd lost us. He must have managed to keep with us somehow.'

'All the same, there's not much he can do now that he's here, is there?' Whacker asked.

'Maybe not,' said Richie. 'But all the same just to have him is great.' And it was great! Just to feel Patchie's warmth against him made all the difference. But it was quite dark now. Even Patchie would not be able to help when Fatser and Ferrety-Face came back.

6 *Robbers in the House*

May had finished cleaning up the passage after Patchie and was crossing the Square to Imelda's house when she saw Mrs. Doyle standing in her doorway, the baby in her arms. The house behind her was in darkness and May guessed that Mr. Doyle had never come back to fix the fuse.

'Are the lights still gone on you, Mrs. Doyle?' she asked.

'Are they what?' came the reply. 'It's black as the divil in there. The ironing's only half done an' I had to bring the babbie out here before I could see to change his nappy. Heaven send you never marry a man that puts his pint before his family. I tell you I'd have him out of that pub faster than a dose of salts only for this lot!'

'I'll mind them for you, Mrs. Doyle,' said May, taking the baby from her arms.

'God bless you, child. You're fit for an earl! I won't be ten minutes gone!' Mrs. Doyle put on her coat and hat and hurried off.

When she came back she had an indignant Mr. Doyle with her. 'It'd serve ya better to check your facts before making accusations agin yer better half before his mates,' he was saying. 'I got no message from ya, good, bad or indifferent.'

'D'ya hear that, May?' called Mrs. Doyle. 'This fella is after swearin' he never laid eyes on that brother of yours this evenin', if we can believe his story!'

'D'ya want your fuse fixed or yer head busted?' enquired Mr. Doyle.

'I'll have the fuse fixed, if it's all the same to you,' said Mrs. Doyle calmly, 'an' if I accused ya in the wrong I apologize, an' I can't do handsomer than that.'

'I'm sorry if Richie let you down, Mrs. Doyle', said May. 'I'm sure if Mr. Doyle says so it's true, though it's not one bit like Richie.'

'Never you mind, child,' said Mrs. Doyle. 'It's not your worry. Yer a grand girl for minding the childer.'

Mr. Doyle nodded 'Get a few sweets for yerself,' he said, slipping a coin into the pocket of May's coat. 'Don't ya know well I wouldn't hurt ya or Mrs. Doyle either – not for the world and Garrett Reilly.'

May told Imelda about it, as they set off for the tobacconist that stayed open late and sold sweets.

Imelda was surprised. 'I seen him go off down the Quays with Whacker,' she said. 'I seen them leavin' the Square.'

'They must be up to somethin' so,' said May, and then forgot about Richie while deciding which sweets to buy with the money Mr. Doyle had given her.

But when her father got back from the pub after closing-time and Richie still wasn't back, May began to worry in earnest. Could he and Whacker have gone back to continue the treasure hunt on their own and maybe been surprised by Fatser and Ferrety-Face? She remembered the bruises on Richie's arms and the way the little man had looked at him. She wondered should she tell her mother about it. Her mother'd skin them for playing on the Market site. But if Richie was in real trouble …? But then again, if he was all right he'd be raging with her for telling!

And there was not only Richie. There was Whacker and Imelda and Mickser to think about as well. She'd be informing on all of them. She could not sleep for worrying about it.

Then she heard her mother's step on the stairs. The door of her room opened. The light on the landing sent a shaft of light across the floor. Her mother looked into the room.

'May! Are ya awake?' she asked. 'D'ya know where that brother of yours could be at this hour of the night?'

May opened her mouth to say, 'Is he not home yet?' and closed it again. She could never tell lies to her mother, even when they were not so much lies as words that would steer her mother away from the truth.

'Well,' her mother went on, 'do ya or don't ya know?'

'I know he was with Whacker,' May said. 'Imelda said she saw them. I know where they mighta gone.'

Her mother looked at her carefully and sighed. She said: 'Ya'd better slip on yer coat and come and tell your Da about it.'

When May went downstairs, Whacker and Imelda's father was there too. May felt awful. There was one thing none of them ever did and that was to tell on someone. Anybody who did that was out for good. Nobody would want to play with them again.

'Well, May,' said her father. 'I'm told ya know where we might start lookin' for Richie and Paddy.'

May knew that when Whacker was called Paddy things were serious, really serious.

'I only thought,' she said awkwardly, 'that they might have gone back to look for the treasure.'

'What treasure?' demanded Whacker's father.

'Ya'd better tell us the whole story,' May's father said. 'If it's a thing that Richie or Paddy might come to harm, it'd be right to tell, even if it's a secret!'

So May told them the whole story, starting from the moment Mickser had broken up the skipping game with his ball. When she got to Fatser and Ferrety-Face and their metal detector, her father looked very worried.

'How often have I warned the lot of yez never to get mixed up in things that don't concern yez,' he said. 'Those boyos are up to no good and they don't sound the kind to go easy on anyone interferin' with their plans. We may have to get the Guards on to this.'

Now May was even more worried. She and Richie usually thought of the Guards as men to be avoided when you were up to devilment, like knocking on doors and running away, or scutting on the back of milk vans or the binmen's carts. When the Guards were on your side it meant they had come with news that someone had been hit by a car or hurt in a brawl outside a pub.

'Maybe first we should take a look at this box they buried in the Square,' said Whacker's father.

'I think we should talk to the Guards first,' said May's father. 'If those two men have got Richie and Paddy there's no time to be lost. May had better come along with us.'

'She can't go out like that,' said her mother. 'She's only pyjamas under her coat.'

'Then put a ganzy on her, quick,' said her father.

So May, wearing a sweater and a coat over her pyjamas, set out with the two men.

The Garda Station was only a few minutes away, round at the back of the Four Courts and, at the pace they hurried May along, they were there in no time.

The sergeant on duty was a big man and May was a bit scared of him. But there was a young garda there who winked at May as she stood there with her pyjamas bottoms showing beneath her coat. The wink made May feel a lot better.

When the sergeant had heard the full story he said to May. 'Would you know those two men again if you saw them?

'Oh yes,' said May. 'I'd see them comin' a mile off.'

'Maybe then you'd have a go at describing them for me?'

May nodded eagerly: 'One's fat with a red face an' great big hands with fingers like sausages. The other's a little scut of a fella with a mean ferrety-face and shifty eyes. He fidgets about all the time he's talkin'.'

The sergeant nodded: 'That's as good a description as ever I had.'

The young garda winked at May once more.

'Did you notice what they were wearing?'

'They'd good overcoats on them,' May said. 'One coat was dark and the other a kind of browny-fawn. I think they were made of tweed.'

The sergeant wrote down everything that May told him. 'You said they had a car. What was that like?'

'Big and black and shiny and new,' said May, 'Whacker said it was a Mercedes 200.'

'We'll circulate the descriptions and see what comes back,' he said. 'Someone may have seen them or know something about them. And you, young lady.' He turned and looked at May: 'How would you like a ride in a squad car?'

He spoke to the young garda: 'Let her cruise around for a while in case she spots anything. Then take her back home. After that, you can try your hand at digging for treasure.'

May felt very important as she got into the squad car. Although she was worried about Richie and Whacker getting home safe, she had a lovely picture in her mind of seeing Ferrety-Face and Fatser and shouting: 'That's them! That's them!'

After that it would be just like the pictures with Ferrety-Face and Fatser running and being caught and having to tell where Richie and Whacker were.

But as the squad car drove slowly up and down the streets between the Quays and Bolton Street she felt very tired. She saw no one who looked in the least like Fatser or Ferrety-Face. Nor was there a car like the big black one that Whacker had said was a Mercedes 200.

In the end, she was rubbing her eyes to try to keep them open and was glad enough to find herself back in the Square, as near to her house as the little row of posts would allow. But as soon as May got out of the warm squad car all the sleepy feeling left her again.

She ran to the door of the house, hoping her mother would say that Richie was back home long ago. But Richie wasn't there. Everyone else was though; Imelda, Mickser, even old Danny Noonan. The front parlour was full of people.

May thought her mother would tell her to go

straight up to bed. But she didn't, so May squeezed into a corner behind the television set with Imelda and told her about the sergeant and the drive in the squad car with the young garda.

Then the young garda himself came in with the box like a house that they had buried in the hole that Patchie had dug. Only then did May realise that Patchie was missing too.

May wondered if she should tell the garda about Patchie in case it was important but she could not get near him with all the people crowding around him to see the box.

The young garda opened the box and took out of it the dirty old pot and plate. 'Can anyone tell me for sure that these are what the children dug up on the Market site?' he asked.

'Yes, that's them!' May and Imelda shouted from their corner.

'We were expectin' something real valuable,' said Mickser. 'A load of ould coins and jewels. Instead we only found those ould yokes! '

Danny Noonan, who had been looking very carefully at the old pot and plate, said slowly and carefully: 'Maybe you found something better than old coins and jewels, young Dolan. The garda here may not agree, but the Derrynaflann Chalice and Patten that's in the Museum now looked much like that when they were first dug up."

The garda nodded: 'That's true, so I'd best take them down to the station and put them under lock

and key. The sergeant will probably inform the National Museum on Monday morning.'

'You mean,' squeaked May, 'that we did find the treasure?'

'Well, I don't know too much about it being treasure,' said the young garda, 'but I'd say this is certainly what those two men in the Mercedes were after.'

For a second May was delighted. That put them one up on Fatser and Ferrety-Face! Then a terrible thought struck her. She said: 'Fatser and Ferrety-Face know we took those things out of the Market.'

There was a stunned silence.

Then May's father spoke: 'Why d'ya say that?'

'Cos all those things were inside a bigger box an' when we took the things, we filled the bigger box with ould stones and lumps of cement. Then we put it back for Fatser and Ferrety-Face to find. They'll know it was us who did it.'

'An' you never said a word about this 'til now,' moaned her mother. 'You're a terrible girl.'

'I only just thought of it when I seen the box,' said May. 'It was Richie's idea anyway to put the stones in the big box. He wanted to make Fatser and Ferrety-Face real mad.'

'Well,' said the young garda gravely, 'I'm afraid mad is what they most likely were ... and probably still are. Let's just hope somebody finds your brother and Whacker before Fatser and Ferrety-Face do.'

7 *Pick it up! Pick it up!*

Inside the old mill it was quite dark now. The only light was the reflection off the surface of the river as it tumbled past before being sucked into the foaming waters that plunged down over the weir.

'What time would you say it was now?' Richie asked.

'I dunno,' said Whacker. 'Around midnight, maybe.'

'Them two'll be back shortly so.' Richie felt Patchie's tongue against his hand. 'Patchie's fed up hangin' around. He wants to go.'

'I think he wants ya to play with him,' said Whacker.

'An' how can I play with him when I'm all tied up?'

'I'll show you,' said Whacker. 'Here, boy! Here!'

Patchie bounded over to him, his head cocked, wagging his tail hopefully. Whacker kicked a stone towards the river.

At once Patchie was after it, seized it, shook it and brought it back to lay at Whacker's feet. Again he looked hopefully up at Whacker's face, his tail still wagging.

'Eegit!' said Whacker, but he kicked it again.

This time Patchie played with the stone as if it

were a rat, tossing it up in the air and catching it again.

'At least HE'S having fun,' said Richie.

'Nothing to the fun we'll have when Ferrety-Face gets back here,' said Whacker bitterly.

Patchie brought the stone over to Richie who automatically held out his hand as far as the rope permitted. For weeks he had been trying to train Patchie to put a ball back in his hand, rather than drop it at his feet. Patchie stood up on his hind legs but Richie's hand was too high. Patchie looked at him questioningly, his head on one side.

'What's he supposed to do, fly?' asked Whacker. But Patchie had discovered a way for himself. He jumped up on to the base of the rusty old wheel and edged around it until he could drop the stone into Richie's outstretched hand.

'Good boy, Patchie!' said Richie, pleased that his training was having such success.

'Pity now, it wasn't a gun he brought ya!' said Whacker.

'Or a knife,' said Richie. "If I'd a knife, I think I could move my wrist enough to cut this rope.'

'How about a sharp-edged stone?' enquired Whacker. 'Old Danny Noonan says the Vikings over at Wood Quay made their knives that way.'

'How would I sharpen it?' asked Richie.

Patchie looked up at his master and wagged his tail. He had gone to a lot of trouble to give back the stone to Richie in the correct way. Now the very least that Richie could do was to throw it for him again.

'There's one here that looks kinda sharp already,' said Whacker. 'If I could only reach it!' He stretched out his leg.

'Patchie'll bring it to you,' said Richie. 'Call him over.'

'Here, Patchie!' Whacker called. 'Here, boy!'

Patchie looked at him and wagged his tail. Then he looked back at Richie again.

'Go to Whacker!' Richie commanded the dog.

'Here, boy,' Whacker called again.

Patchie bounded over to Whacker, watching him closely. Whacker kicked out at the stone and managed to move it. It didn't go very far but Patchie decided it was better than nothing. He picked it up and carried it back to Whacker.

'No!' Richie called. 'Bring it to me! Here boy! Here!'

Patchie looked at him quizically. He was reluctant to go to so much trouble a second time. But Richie held out his hand.

'Here!' he said. 'Here, Patchie! Good boy!'

Patchie gave him a long searching look, and Richie's heart sank.

Then suddenly Patchie hopped up on to the wheel once more and dropped the stone into Richie's outstretched hand.

'Good dog,' cried Richie and Whacker together, and Patchie wagged his tail harder than ever, delighted by such praise.

'Is it sharp enough?' asked Whacker.

'I dunno,' said Richie, 'but I'll have a go.'

He twisted the stone until the rough edge was away from his palm and began to chafe it against the strands of the rope. Whacker and Patchie watched impatiently.

'Any good?' enquired Whacker, trying to stay calm.

'It's gonna take ages to cut it like this,' said Richie, 'and my wrists are achin' like anything.'

'You'll ache in a lot more places if Ferrety-Face has his way,' Whacker retorted.

There was no arguing with that, so Richie gritted his teeth and kept going. After a while he felt a strand of rope giving.

'It's working!' he cried joyfully.

'Can you get yer arm free?' asked Whacker.

'Not yet,' said Richie.

'Well, don't take all night over it,' said Whacker.

'I'm doin' the best I can. You'll only have to be patient.' Suddenly Richie felt the second strand give. He flexed his muscles and strained at the last remaining strand. Sweat broke out on his forehead from the effort and the pain. Then, at last, the coil of rope went slack.

'I've done it!' he said, hardly able to believe it.

'Then for the love of God come and untie me and let's get outa this!' said Whacker.

Richie struggled free and stumbled over to

Whacker. He felt weak now, almost giddy. There were pins and needles in his right arm.

'What's wrong now?' Whacker demanded. 'Can't you get the knot untied?'

'I'm stiff,' Richie said, 'from being tied up all that time. Now I've pins and needles!' He held out his hand and opened it and closed it a few times, trying to get it working again. It would be awful if Fatser and Ferrety-Face were to get back before they were clear away! He tried the knot again. This time it opened. Whacker was free!

They hurried away from the dripping pillar and the roar of the weir towards the dim light ahead. Suddenly they found themselves facing the outside world. A crescent moon riding high through the clouds cast its light on the grass that spread in front of them like a carpet. It was as though they'd been released from gaol after a long sentence. Patchie gave a joyous bark.

'Hush, Patchie,' said Richie. 'We don't want them two down on top of us.' He looked around. A track led from the mill towards a bridge which hung in a dark arc to their right. Near the bridge was a gate and beside the gate was a cottage. It was like the one at the entrance to the Botanical Gardens. Richie guessed that must be where Fatser and Ferrety-Face were eating their supper.

Beside the gatehouse was another huge building, very like the one they had just escaped from. On one side of it, and almost a third of its height, was a giant water-mill. Behind it flowed the second branch of the river. The boys stared in surprise at the reflection of the moon where they had expected solid ground.

'We're on some kind of an island,' Richie said.

To their left they could see an old house, solid and four square, with a belt of trees behind it. The millowner must have lived there once upon a time, when both mills were grinding away, supplying flour to the Georgian city of Dublin.

But the track from the gate stopped at a wide sweep in front of the house. Between the trees moonlight glittered on more water. The two branches of the river must meet beyond the house. The only way off the island was up the steep slope and through the gate on to the bridge. To get there they had to pass the gatehouse.

'If we hear them comin' out,' Richie said, 'we can duck into the other mill there by the gate 'til they've passed. Then we can make a run for it.'

Whacker nodded. 'Come on then,' he said. They set off across the grass towards the track that ran past the gatehouse. Patchie kept close to their heels, like a small shadow.

They hurried as fast as they could, but their limbs were still cramped from being tied up for so long and they were both hobbling like old Danny Noonan as they reached the track. They had less than a hundred yards to go to the gate when suddenly Patchie gave a long low warning growl. The door of the gatehouse opened and the two men came out.

'What now?' gasped Whacker. 'We're too far from the mill! We'll never make it before they see us!'

'Run!' said Richie. 'This way!' and the boys turned and ran as hard as they could away from the gatehouse, and also away from the bridge and freedom.

A shout from behind them told them they had been seen!

'Where are we goin'?' panted Whacker, as they raced up the driveway towards the house.

'Maybe we can dodge in among the trees and then double back,' gasped Richie.

That seemed to be the only hope. The boys had a fair start and the distance between them and the men would have been even greater if the boys had not been so stiff. Indeed they could easily have got away but for the fact that they were running in the wrong direction. Soon there would be nothing ahead of them but the river.

Patchie was the only one enjoying the chase! He kept bounding in front of the boys and then racing back again by way of encouragement. At last they reached the belt of trees and plunged in. Then in front of them they saw the weir.

They both stared at it in surprise. From the sound echoing through the old mill, they had imagined it to be close to the old mill-wheel. The

river running between the two high stone walls must have funnelled the sound back into the echoing mill, for there was the weir beyond the sheltering trees and, beyond it again, yet another island. Barely fifty yards across, it straddled the river so that only a narrow channel separated it from the bank.

'If we only could get over to the small island,' said Richie, 'I think we could get across to the far bank.'

'You're out of your skull!' said Whacker. 'We could never get across THAT!' He pointed, horrified, at the water that foamed and crashed down over the weir.

'It's our only chance,' said Richie.

Looking around, Richie saw a tree branch hanging out over the weir. He tested it and then swung out on it the way he used to swing on a rope tied to a lamp-post, performing feats like 'the duck' and 'the wild man'. Patchie stood at the water's edge and barked frantically as Richie dropped gently down on to the weir. For a second he almost fell but then, using his arms like wings to keep his balance, he began to make his way towards the little island.

Patchie sprang into the water and began to swim after him. But the pull of the weir was too strong and he was swept away, struggling wildly, Richie watched, terrified that the dog would be drowned. Then he realised that the current was carrying Patchie towards the tip of the island.

'Patchie's all right,' Richie called to Whacker,

who still hesitated by a rock. 'Swing out on the branch.'

Whacker still did not move. Then Ferrety-Face appeared between the trees. Whacker hesitated no longer. He grabbed the branch, closed his eyes, and swung out over the weir.

Whacker landed awkwardly, putting his right foot in a pool of frothing water, but by grabbing an iron post that stuck up out of the river he managed to haul himself up to the top of the weir. Then he followed Richie quickly to the other side of it. There was a gap there that separated it from the small island. Without saying a word, they both jumped out across the gap but, instead of landing on firm ground, they sank in soft ooze almost up to their knees.

'Yuk!' said Whacker, 'This place is all mud!'

Richie pointed at the projecting roots of the shrubs that covered most of the island: 'Grab a hold of those and pull yourself up the bank.'

Within seconds they were standing on solid ground.

Almost at once a wet bundle of fur came bounding up to them from the far end of the island. It was Patchie, none the worse for his swim.

The boys glanced back across the weir. Fatser and Ferrety-Face were standing at the edge of the wild tossing water and shouting at each other. They were obviously having an argument.

'Fatser wants Ferrety-Face to swing across the

way we did, and Ferrety-Face won't!' grinned Richie.

'I hope he tries it!' Whacker grinned back. 'That branch would never be strong enough to hold him!'

Suddenly the two men turned and ran back among the trees.

"I bet you they've gone for the van,' said Whacker, 'They'll try to head us off at the road. We'd better not hang around here!'

The boys hurried to the northern side of the island.

'Watch out for the mud!' warned Whacker.

'We can go by the rocks there!' shouted Richie as they reached the water's edge once more.

The channel here was wider than they had expected. There was no chance of jumping across.

'It's not that deep,' said Richie.

'There's three feet of water with four feet of mud under that,' Whacker calculated. 'I wouldn't like to try wadin' through that lot!'

'Then we'll have to swim it,' said Richie.

Once more Whacker looked at him in horror. 'Ya can't even do the length of the Iveagh Baths and ya wanta swim this?'

Richie grinned: 'This is less than the width of the Baths. We ought to be able to manage that.'

'And what about the current?'

'No current this side of the island. Look.' Richie threw a small stick into the water. It floated gently down the river, hardly seeming to move. 'There's no current at all.'

Richie took off his boots, tied the laces together and hung them around his neck. They were thick with mud, but then so was he. He grinned at Whacker. 'Bet I'm first across,' he said.

'You're on,' said Whacker, pulling off his boots.

They plunged into the river with Patchie right behind them. In the event it was Patchie who won the contest and stood barking on the bank as the boys stumbled ashore, coughing and spluttering from the dirty water they had swallowed.

As soon as they had managed to force their wet feet back into their boots Whacker said: 'We can't stand here shiverin'. Them two'll be around here in the van in jig time. We've got to get out of here fast. Over there maybe.' Whacker raised his hand and pointed up the river bank towards the darkness of the Phoenix Park.

8 *Kick them out! Kick them out!*

When Maura Reilly heard that Richie and Whacker were missing, she felt awful! She was sure it had something to do with the hunt for the treasure and with those two awful men who had tried to chase them off the site.

'What d'ya think happened them?' she asked her mother.

'How do I know? Go to yer bed,' her mother replied.

'I hope they're not hurted,' said Maura, remembering the way that Fatser had spread out his fat sausage-fingers, as if he longed to squeeze them around Richie's throat. 'Are they all out lookin' for them?'

'Your father's goin' across to Byrnes now,' said her mother.

'Can I go with him?' asked Maura.

'Such notions!' said her mother. 'This is a job for the men. Go to bed now! Ya should have been asleep long ago.'

But Maura could not sleep. If she had gone back to the gap in the hoarding that second night with the others she might now know where Richie and Whacker were. She might still be in on the secret. 'If anything happens to Richie and Whacker,' she thought, 'I might get the blame for not being there to keep cavey. May and Imelda will be black out with me for ever.'

She waited until she heard her mother go out the back. Then she took her gaberdine off the hook and slipped out into the darkness of the Square.

She could see the light in the front parlour window of the Byrne house across the Square. But it was no use going there. Her father would only send her home again. She turned away from the lights and walked towards St. Mary's Abbey.

Over in the Byrne's front parlour, after the young garda had taken the chalice and patten in their house-shaped box back to the station, the men began organizing themselves into search parties. Richie and May's father and Whacker and Imelda's father would search the area north of the Square, as far as Phibsboro. Mickser's father and brother would cover the roads to the east, all the way up to the Docks. Mr. Doyle and another neighbour would go east as far as Heuston Bridge. The lads who lived next to the Doyles would take the other side of the river. Old Danny Noonan wanted to join the search too, but everyone said he'd be too slow and would only delay everyone.

After the men had set out, May was sure that her mother would send her to bed. But she didn't. Instead she said: 'I'm running across to poor Kathleen.'

Kathleen was Whacker and Imelda's mother.

'Stay here and keep an eye on the young lads for me. Ya can make a sup of tea for Danny an' anyone else that drops in. An' if there's any news, you or Imelda run over and tell us.'

'We will of course,' the two girls assured her, feeling important and responsible again.

Meanwhile, Maura was trudging up Mary's Lane towards Church Street. She did not really know why, except that she had already searched St. Mary's Abbey and Meeting House Lane. She had even peeped in through the gap in the hoarding, but all had been silent inside the old Markets. That it was also empty Maura could see by the moonlight that shone through the space where the roof had been. Then she remembered Fatser and Ferrety-Face driving off along Mary's Lane in their car so she set off in that direction, pulling her gaberdine tightly around her against the cold.

■

Richie and Whacker felt the cold as well as they ran across the Chapelizod road and scaled the Park railings. Then they raced for the shelter of the trees that lined the southern edge of the Park. Patchie ran ahead of them, pausing occasionally to sniff the air as if looking for signs of danger.

At the base of the Wellington Monument, that stood dark and cold against the cloud-scattered sky, the two boys and the dog paused. The main road of the Park was deserted. Faint lights flickered from thin green lamp-standards. It was like being caught in a dream.

Whacker shivered, whether from the cold or not he didn't know. 'We should make for the main gate,' he said. 'From there we can follow the river and be back in the Square in no time.'

Richie shook his head: 'That's exactly what Fatser and Ferrety-Face'll expect us to do. We gotta stick to the back streets!'

Whacker groaned. He had hurt his foot landing in the pool by the weir. Walking in wet boots had made it worse.

'We'll go up by Arbour Hill,' said Richie 'an' into North King Street.'

Whacker groaned again: 'North King Street's miles away.'

Richie nodded: 'That's why it's the last place them two will look for us. An' anyway there's loads of little streets an' alleyways and shop-doorways we can duck into once we get there. It's the only safe way, Whacker. Come on.'

■

Maura turned into Church Street, past the old St. Michan's, the Protestant St. Michan's, where people went to see the bodies. She shivered at the thought of people lying dead in the crypt for hundred of years with the flesh still on them. like the vampires in the picture she had once seen on the telly. She had never had the courage to go into St. Michan's herself, but Whacker had been. She remembered him boasting of how he had shaken the

hand of the one they called The Crusader. She did not like to think about such things, alone in the middle of the night, with moonlight striking the square tower of the church. The sound of her footsteps seemed to echo back from the tower. They were very loud in the stillness of the night. It was terrible, being all on her own. Of course it would be worse if she heard another set of footsteps behind her, not knowing who or what was following her! She moved quickly into Hammond Lane.

Suddenly a van, just like the one that belonged to the wallpaper shop in Capel Street, was coming towards her.

At the sight of her the van began to slow down. At once Maura felt more afraid of the van than of all the spirits that might haunt the old crypt and churchyard at St. Michan's. For there, at the wheel, was Fatser and, in the seat beside him, the little edgy figure of Ferrety-Face!

Maura ran towards the van, knowing that the lane was too narrow for it to turn, and dashed past it. She did not stop to think where she was going but just ran and ran until she found herself in a street almost as wide as the Square. Only then did she realise that she was lost! But she did not dare to stop even though she was getting a stitch in her side. She turned another corner. Two men were coming towards her. She screamed out in terror. Then she burst into tears. The two men were May's father and Imelda's father.

∎

Richie and Whacker trudged on passed Arbour Hill Barracks. They were tired. Their feet hurt. They were scared even to talk in case they missed the first warning sound of a van in low gear climbing the hill behind them. This part of the journey was the most exposed, with only the bare railings beside them. Beyond the railings they could see the grass and paving stones in front of the gold cross on the wall that marked the graves of the leaders of the 1916 Rising.

Arbour Hill was silent in the same way that the Park had been. When they first left the Park it had been all right. There were trucks close by, moving along the Dublin-Galway road, and it seemed too public a place for Fatser and Ferrety-Face to try to recapture them.

But now Arbour Hill seemed full of danger and when a dog, suddenly aware of Patchie who was trotting at their side, barked loudly in a neighbouring house, they jumped as if Fatser and Ferrety-Face were upon them.

Only when they reached the first of the small roads of little houses between Arbour Hill and Stoneybatter did they feel safe again.

'I've gotta stop for a while,' gasped Whacker.

Richie looked at him, worried: 'We can't stop yet.'

'Well, I've gotta,' Whacker said in such a way that Richie knew he meant it.

Richie had always thought of Whacker as being stronger than himself. Now he realised that Whacker's heavier build and broad shoulders were almost too much for his legs to carry. Richie's own thin, wiry body seemed to have suffered much less from the cold and hunger and the sheer effort they had put into escaping.

'All right then. Five minutes. But not here.'

They turned the corner into a side street. Whacker gripped the wall for support. He looked very pale. Richie said nothing, only put an arm around Whacker's shoulder as they both sat down on the edge of the path.

'He's not gonna last much longer,' Richie thought. 'An' we've the best part of a mile to go yet!'

■

When Maura was able to talk clearly enough for the two fathers to understand her, she told them why she had been running out of Smithfield. She expected them to laugh or to be angry with her. But instead they were as worried as she herself had been about the van.

'What class of a van were they driving?'

'One like the one belonging to the wallpaper shop in Capel Street,' Maura said.

'That's a Renault 4L,' Richie's father said. 'What colour?'

'The same as the wallpaper shop, red.'

'Good girl yerself!' said Richie's father. 'Come

on, 'til we tell the Guards about it.'

'The Guards?' Maura echoed stupidly.

Whacker's father nodded: 'The Guards'll have a better chance of catchin' them if they know they're in a red van. At present they're lookin' for a black Mercedes 200.'

∎

The two boys trudged on.

When Richie saw the traffic lights at the top of Church Street, his heart lifted. They could cut through any of the little roads into Beresford Street and in a few seconds be in Mary's Lane.

'Nearly there now,' he said to Whacker.

Whacker did not answer or even smile. He just kept stumbling on, putting one foot in front of the other, guided by Richie's arm. It was as if he could neither see nor hear, but only keep moving in the direction which Richie pointed him.

They passed the Father Mathew Hall and began to cross the road. Patchie's tail wagged wearily. He was pleased to be so close to home.

Then the red van swung out of one of the side streets and headed straight for them.

The boys stopped, frozen.

The van pulled up with a screeching of brakes. Out of it jumped Ferrety-Face and Fatser. They grabbed the two boys and began to drag them towards the van. Richie tried to struggle.

Then the air was filled with a police-car siren.

At once Ferrety-Face let go of Richie and ran for

the van with Patchie snapping at his heels. Richie turned to see Whacker fall to the ground as Fatser let go of him. Then the police car came around the corner from Chancery Street, blocking the van's way forward.

Fatser at once threw the van into reverse, heading directly for where Whacker lay motionless on the ground. Richie started to run towards it, shouting for the van to stop, shouting that Whacker would surely be killed.

Then he felt a blinding pain and everything went blank.

■

When he opened his eyes again, Richie did not know where he was. He felt as if he were an insect inside a cocoon. His head ached. There were curtains all round him.

Then he remembered Whacker lying in the path of the van. He tried to speak.

'Take it easy, son.' It was his mother's voice. He turned his head and there she was seated on a chair beside him.

Richie opened his mouth again and his voice came out all funny. 'Whacker?' he managed to croak.

'Not a bother on him. They're lettin' him up this morning. Ya won't be long after him yerself.'

Richie spoke again. This time his voice sounded all right: 'Where am I? What happened?'

'Yer in Jervis Street Hospital, son. Ya tried to

stop the van from runnin' over Whacker and ya got knocked down!

'What happened to Fatser and Ferrety-Face?'

'Them two buckoos are under lock and key. An' the Sergeant says ya.'ll be getting a reward for findin' the treasure. That black lookin' pot you buried in the Square is solid silver an' hundreds of years old.'

'Doesn't that beat all,' gasped Richie. 'An' we swearin' blind we never found any treasure at all!'

He thought in silence for a moment. Then he asked: 'What kind of a reward would it be? Would it be money?'

'I dunno, son. Of course, it'll be split up between the lot of ye.'

'But if it was money, how much might it be?'

His mother smiled: 'Enough maybe, to buy that bike ya've been wantin'.'

'Wow!' said Richie. A long time ago he'd seen the bike in the window of The Cycle King on Bachelor's Walk and dreamed ever since of owning it!

Then he thought of something else. 'The squad car?' he asked. 'How did it get there, just when it was needed?'

'Ya can thank Maura Reilly for that,' his mother said. 'Maura told the Guards.'

'Maura?' Richie couldn't fit her into the picture at all.

'Seemingly she went out looking for yez, all on

her own, and saw them in the red van.'

Richie tried to picture white-faced Maura in her worn gaberdine playing detective along the dark quays and streets north of the Liffey. 'We left her out of it,' he said, 'on account of her being such a scaredy cat.'

'Well, ya can count her in from this out,' said his mother. 'Only for her, the guards wouldn'ta put much pass on the van at all.'

'Well, that beats all,' said Richie.

'An' old Danny Noonan says there'll be men from the museum down now to dig up th' ould Abbey, in case there'd be any more pots there like the one yez found.'

'They'd want to listen to the skippin' songs before they start diggin'.' Richie grinned. 'All the clues to where the treasure was hid was in May's skippin' song. She only turned the stone because it had three chips cut in it. The ould plate in the song was the treasure, the silver plate. And Fatser and Ferrety-Face were the robbers in the house.'

'Them two buckoos weren't even born when that song was first sung.' said his mother. 'My mother sang it and her mother before her sang it, so the two in the van couldn't be the robbers in the song.'

'Then the robbers must be Henry the Eighth's soldiers,' said Richie excitedly, 'Danny Noonan told us how Henry the Eighth wrecked the Abbey. The monks musta hidden their treasure to prevent the soldiers from findin' it. They left the clue to where it was in the words of the song.'

'An' yez could well be right,' said his mother, 'for it's not today nor yesterday that that song was made.'

■

When the reward money was divided among the gang there was enough to buy them a bike each.

There was even enough left over to have a party for everyone in the Square. On the Saturday of the party the sun shone down out of a clear blue sky. The men carried tables and chairs out into the middle of the Square. Soon the place looked like a grand open air cafe with lots to eat and drink.

Reporters from the city newspapers, even a television crew, came to the Square. Everyone was interviewed and photographed.

'We'll be famous,' said Imelda, 'People will want our autographs.'

'As long as they don't want me new bike,' said Whacker, 'I won't complain.'

'What about three cheers for Maura?' said Richie, 'Only for her ...' He didn't finish. And as the cheers went up, he added: 'An' for ould Patchie, too, of course.'

And Patchie gave a little bark as much as to say: 'Dead right too, ould son.'

Carolyn Swift

Carolyn Swift has worked in most Dublin theatres, including the Olympia, either as actress, stage-manager or producer, and for ten years ran a small theatre in partnership with her husband. For the stage she wrote seven revues, a rock musical and puppet plays, as well as plays and series for radio and television, including *Wanderly Wagon*, *Bosco* and *Fortycoats*.

She is a regular contributer to Radio Éireann's Sunday morning programme, *Sunday Miscellany*.

Robbers in the House

Robbers in the Hills

Robbers in the Town

Robbers in the Theatre